Adventures of
Apple & Banana
Aisle of the Cookies

D.J. Mincy

Outskirts Press, Inc.
Denver, Colorado

Adventures of Apple & Banana
Aisle of the Cookies
All Rights Reserved.
Copyright © 2010 D.J. Mincy
V2.0 R1.4

Cover Photo © 2010 JupiterImages Corporation. All rights reserved - used with permission.

Outskirts Press, Inc.
http://www.outskirtspress.com

ISBN: 978-1-4327-5204-0

Outskirts Press and the "OP" logo are trademarks belonging to Outskirts Press, Inc.

PRINTED IN THE UNITED STATES OF AMERICA

Chapter 1

The moon full and bright seemed to smile down on the Safe & Fresh Grocery store. Inside the store, the lights turned off one by one. A teenage girl locked up the front doors.

"Alice!" A high pitched voice called from the back of the store. "Alice are you' almost done locking up?" Mr. Wigley, the store manager, said in an impatient voice.

Alice rolled her eyes and ignored Mr. Wigley's question and continued locking up the last of the doors.

Mr. Wigley wobbled down the cereal and bread aisle towards Alice, his massive head bobbled back and forth.

"Alice! Alice! Did you hear me?"

"Mr. Wigley did you say something?" Alice said with a smile on her face.

"You know darn well that you heard me," he said in a high-pitched voice.

Alice smiled and thought Mr. Wigley's voice sounded like a cat who got its tail stepped on.

She smiled broadly when Mr. Wigley stood in front of her with his arms on the side of his hips. He reminded her of Grimace, and if she just painted him purple. Alice giggled at the thought.

"Relax, Mr. Wigley, it's time to go home," Alice said.

Mr. Wigley took his hands off his hips.

Mr. Wigley huffed. "Yeah I am glad to get out of here tonight. All those crazy shoppers in here. I blame the full moon," he said.

"Maybe it's the full moon, Mr. Wigley. All the doors are locked. So let's get out of here," Alice said.

"Okay, let me just set the alarm," Mr. Wigley said as he punched in the code on the alarms keypad.

The alarm beeped several times alerting them they had to leave the store quickly.

As Alice and Mr. Wigley walked out towards the cars, Mr. Wigley glared at the moon.

"Why are you so happy?" He said as he shook his fist angrily at the moon.

Boy, he is crazy, Alice thought.

"Good night Mr. Wigley," Alice said in a cheerful voice.

"Good night Alice. See you tomorrow morning," Mr. Wigley said.

Alice shook her head. "Not tomorrow. I am off this weekend. I will be in on Monday," she said.

Mr. Wigley was about to express his displeasure to Alice, but she had already gotten in her car and drove off.

Before Mr. Wigley got into his car, he looked disapprovingly at the moon again.

After Mr. Wigley left the parking lot the moonlight twinkled thru the windows of the Safe and Fresh Store. Only pockets of moonlight illuminated portions of the store.

As the time hit 11:11, the inside of the Safe and Fresh store began to glow with a bright blue and white intense light. The store grew larger and larger, and the ceiling began to disappear along with any recognition of the aisles of food.

The flashing blue and white lights continued. A strange and mysterious world began to take form. This new world seemed to be painted by some invisible divine power.

As the new world began to take shape the Safe and Fresh store slowly began to disappear only a small part of the store in the bakery and produce aisle remained. Phantom voices and children's laughter echoed throughout the eerily empty store.

With one last burst of blue light, the last of the Safe and Fresh store disappeared and was replaced by a strange and mysterious place. Where the bakery and produce aisle use to be, several overturned trays of doughnuts lay.

"Shhh! You will wake up the bread," a child's voice said.

The laughter stopped.

"Yeah whatever lets wake up the bread! Yippee!" Said a banana swinging on a make shift rope and crashing into a tray of doughnuts.

"Zachary Banana Slick stop goofing off you are going to get us caught," a chubby red apple with short stubby legs said.

Zachary with a large cheesy grin strolled over to the irritated apple.

"Relax Edward Apple Edison. You are always up-tight. Let's have some fun," the brash Zachary said as he slapped Edward on his back.

Edward considered what Zachary said and shook his head and smiled. "I am not that uptight," he said.

"Yeah right you are as tight as a jar of pickles and look at your shirt," Zachary said.

"What about my shirt?" Edward said in a defensive voice.

"Must you have your last name printed on it? EDISON," Zachary said as he laughed.

"Whatever, what do you want to do today?" Edward asked.

Zachary picked up a large doughnut and started twirling it around him like a hula-hoop.

"Yeah baby! This is how you do it," Zachary said as he spun the doughnut faster and faster around him.

"Zachary what do you want to do?" Edward asked again.

Zachary stopped, and his mischievous eyes sparkled. "Let's get out of here," he said.

"Out of where?" Edward replied, confused by Zachary's strange request.

"Let's blow this doughnut stand," Zachary said.

Edward was still confused. "What are you talking about?" He said.

Zachary shook his head at Edward. "Some fruits call you a genius, but for a Brainiac you can be quite thick. I am talking about getting out of Safe and Fresh village," Zachary said.

Edward took a step away from Zachary his mouth wide open.

"Are you kidding me we never left the village by ourselves," Edward said.

"Right on my well rounded friend. Haven't you ever

thought of what adventures we can get into?" Zachary asked.

Edward thought for a moment. "Well yeah but this is dangerous thinking," he said.

"Well you know me dangerous is my middle name," Zachary said as he puffed out his canary yellow chest.

"If we are to leave where would we go?" Edward asked.

"To the Aisle of Cookies," Zachary said as he emphatically threw up his arms as if he was signaling a touchdown.

Edwards stared at Zachary in horror. "Are you crazy? Loco in the cabasa? You crazy fruit! No one's ever returned from the Aisle of the Cookies," Edward said.

"Those are just rumors. Besides who do you know that's tried to go there?" Zachary quizzed.

Edward shrugged his shoulders.

"Exactly no one, we could be the first. Come on Edward let's do this. Or are you scared? Are you a chicken nugget? Are you shaking in your red skin?" Zachary said teasing his best friend.

"I am not scared!" Edward said trying to hide his fear.

"No, you're not scared? Why does your face look like you have to go poop some apple seeds?"

Edward glared at Zachary. "Okay I will go!" He said in a high pitch voice.

"Really? Are you sure? It's going to be awesome Edward."

"I hope we make it back alive," Edward said under his breath.

"Stop being so stupid and let's do this. You're the brains here.

How do we get to Aisle of Cookies?" Zachary asked.

Edward thought for a moment. He had some knowledge of this mythical place but finding the Aisle of Cookies would be like finding a needle in a haystack.

"I believe we head north towards Fruit City," Edward said.

"Fruit City!" Zachary said as he jumped around.

"Don't get too excited slim we are only heading in that direction," Edward said.

"I remember going to Fruit City when I was a kid," Zachary said.

"You're still a kid mush head," Edward said.

"I am bigger kid now," Zachary said trying to defend himself.

"Yeah with a bigger mouth, Edward added.

Zachary was about to come back at Edward when a voice called out from behind them.

"Hi, boys," a girl's voice said.

Edward and Zachary turned around to see Ava Pretini and next to her Alex N. Charge.

Ava and Alex were Edward and Zachary's school friends.

"Hi Ava," Edward said in a bashful voice.

Ava was bright and physically in shape. Her dad always challenged her to eat well and take care of her mind and body. She was friendly but had a tuff side to her. Many of the children in school respected her.

"Hi Edward, what are you boys up to?" Ava asked.

Edward was about to respond when Zachary interrupted.

"Hey Ava you going to say hi to me?" Zachary said as he jumped in front of Edward.

"Of course Zachary, how are you doing?"

"Glad you asked. I am fantastic," Zachary replied.

Zachary turned to Alex with a smirk. "What's up tall and gruesome? Oh sorry you're not tall," Zachary said.

"I will take that peel right off you," Alex said as he started to chase Zachary.

Many kids considered Alex the most athletic in school. Alex caught up to Zachary and had him in a headlock.

As Alex and Zachary wrestled, Ava turned to Edward.

"So what are you guys doing?" She asked.

Edward shook his head because he realized what he was about to say sounded stupid.

"Zachary wanted to go on an adventure," Edward said.

"Adventure to where?" Ava asked.

Edward turned away from Ava, embarrassed.

"He wants to find the Aisle of Cookies," Edward said.

"The Aisle of Cookies!" Ava exclaimed.

Alex had stopped wrestling with Zachary, when he heard Edward.

Edward continued. "I know it sounds like a stupid idea. I..."

Ava cut Edward off.

"Sounds like an awesome adventure," Ava said. "I have heard all kinds of stories about the Aisle of Cookies. Not sure if the stories are true are not but I think we should find out." Ava said as she clapped her hands in excitement.

Alex walked over to Ava and Edward.

"What do you think? Sounds like a brilliant idea," Ava said to Alex.

"I am down. Surprised screw head over here came up with such a terrific idea," Alex said pointing at Zachary.

Zachary strutted over to his three friends.

"So, are you guys in?" Zachary asked Ava and Alex.

"Absolutely!" They said in unison.

"So where do we start?" Alex asked.

"Edward said we go in the direction of Fruit City," Zachary said.

"Let's go," Ava said.

Edward was glad his three best friends would be on this adventure with him.

Edward put his hand out and the other three fruits but their hands on his.

"We are off to the Aisle of Cookies!" Edward said in a surprisingly loud and excited voice.

The four friends raised their hands up and cheered. They headed in the direction of Fruit City, on their way to find the mysterious Aisle of Cookies.

Chapter 2

The four friends left the village and headed to Fruit City.

"Hey how far is Fruit City?" Alex asked.

"Not far we jump on the bus, and we should be there in no time," Edward said.

"How are we going to pay?" Zachary asked Edward.

Edward grinned. "Oh I don't know maybe we can sneak on," he said.

"Really! You want us to sneak on. That's way cool. I am in," Zachary said as he jumped up and down.

"Relax Slick. We are not going to sneak on. I have bus passes," Edward held the bus passes up in his hands.

"I wanted to sneak on," Zachary whined.

"Edward, where did you get the tickets?" Ava asked.

"I go every once in a while with my parents to the city. We go to the museums and libraries," Edward said.

"Boring!" Zachary remarked as he put his hand to his mouth, pretending to yawn.

The four friends walked to the bus stop.

"Have all of you been to the big city?" Alex asked.

Ava, Edward and Zachary nodded their heads.

"Haven't you?" Ava asked.

"No, this will be my first time," he said nervously.

"Oh, is the big bad Alex scared?" Zachary teased.

"Not scared, anxious. I heard all kinds of things happen in the city," said Alex.

"It's not much different than the village, only bigger. Lots of neat things to do in the city and besides Alex we are not actually having our adventure in the city. We can do that some other time," Edward said.

"So we are not going to Fruit City?" Ava asked Edward.

"No, we are going past Fruit City," Edward replied.

"What! You lost your seeds! Do you even know how to get to the Aisle of Cookies? I bet you don't," Zachary chided.

Ava turned to Edward. "Do you know how to get to the Aisle of Cookies?" She asked.

Edward thought for a moment before speaking. "No one knows how to get to the Aisle of Cookies, but I have read many books. I once saw an old map tucked away in a far corner of the basement. The map seemed strange and ancient," Edward stopped and rubbed his chin.

"What was on the map?" Zachary quizzed.

"I believe the map is to the Aisle of Cookies," Edward said proudly.

"You never told me about the map. Why not?" Zachary said as he gave Edward incredulous look.

"Because you would tease me, and call me a nerd," Edward said.

Zachary patted Edward on his back. "How true my brainy friend," Zachary said.

"So you think you can get us to the Aisle of Cookies?" Alex asked.

"I can't promise you anything. The adventure is to look for the Aisle of Cookies. If we don't find the Aisle of Cookies I'm sure we will have fun anyway. Am I right?" Edward said to his three friends.

They all nodded in agreement to Edward.

The bus pulled up. Edward handed each of his friend's bus passes. The four of them excitedly boarded the bus. Edward instructed them to sit in front of the bus. He wanted to make sure they quickly got off the bus, he did not want them missing their stop.

The bus driver, a large avocado, greeted them as they boarded.

"Greetings," he said in a loud cheery voice.

The bus filled with all kinds of different fruits, some large, small, old and young.

"This is awesome!" Ava said as she watched the other fruits on the bus.

Zachary agreed. "I love riding the bus. Good thinking buddy," he said to Edward.

Edward and Ava sat on one side of the bus, Alex and Zachary sat across from them.

The four of them stared out of their windows as the bus headed towards Fruit City.

The bus roared down the street, and made periodic stops to pick up more passengers.

Alex pointed to a variety of large buildings on the horizon. "Is that Fruit City?" He asked.

"That's it," Edward confirmed.

Alex eyes widened. "Wow!"

The four of them marveled at the size of Fruit City.

"Fruit City is so busy and noisy. I love it!" Zachary declared.

Ava turned to Edward. "I do love coming here. I know we can't stop, but I love to ride through here," she said.

Edward agreed with Ava.

The sights and smells of the city captivated them.

A dinging sound vibrated through the bus. The bus slowed down and came to a stop.

"Did you hear a sound?" Alex asked.

"The sound happens when one of the passengers pulls on a rope above which alerts the bus driver someone wants to get off," Edward explained.

Several passengers got off the bus and headed onto the street.

"Next stop downtown," the bus driver bellowed.

"Downtown is the heart of the city," Zachary said to Alex.

The bus slowed down again.

"Here we are, downtown," said the bus driver.

Several more fruits got off the bus leaving only a few

passengers left.

The bus continued on its path making a couple of more stops. Only an elderly male grapefruit was left.

The bus driver turned to the four friends. "Did you guys miss your stop?" The bus driver questioned. "We are leaving Fruit City and only a few stops are left," he said.

Edward assured the bus driver they had not missed their stop. The bus driver continued until he came to the last stop on the bus route.

"I am not even sure why this is a stop. No one ever gets off here, not much around," the bus driver said.

The bus driver had been right. No buildings, villages, towns or cities. Only an open field and large trees greeted them.

"You guys must be going on a hike or something," the bus driver said.

Alex was about to tell the bus driver, but Zachary elbowed him to be quiet.

The four friends got off the bus and thanked the bus driver. The bus driver waved goodbye and turned the bus around and headed off in the direction of Fruit City.

Chapter 3

T he four of them did not detect an old grapefruit behind them.

"Hi, kids, where are you off to?"

The four friends jumped when they heard the old fruit's voice.

"Where did you come from? You scared the seeds out of us," Zachary said.

The old wrinkled-up grapefruit smiled.

"Sorry, young fellow. I was on the bus with you. Allow me to introduce myself. I am Ebenezer Grapefruit."

The old grapefruit gave them a bow.

"Please to meet you Mr. Grapefruit," I am Ava Pretini and these are my friends.

Alex and Edward said hello to Ebenezer, but Zachary eyed him carefully.

"This is Zachary, he is a little suspicious," Edward said.

"As he should be," Ebenezer said.

"So you must be following us. Why would you get off at the last stop at the same time we are?" Zachary said suspiciously.

"I can't go for a stroll and take in the beautiful scenery like you guys? That is what you are doing, going for a stroll?"

"Ah, yeah, we are going on a nature walk," Zachary said.

"Good, well enjoy your walk," Ebenezer said.

The four friends waved goodbye to Ebenezer and started walking. They had walked several feet when Ebenezer shouted to them.

"Be careful when you go to the Aisle of Cookies!"

The four friends stopped and stared at each other.

"How does he know we are going to Aisle of Cookies," Edward whispered to his friends.

They turned around. Ebenezer Grapefruit stood right behind them.

The four friends jumped at Ebenezer being so close to them.

"What a minute you were way over there," Alex said pointing.

"How did you get here so fast?" Zachary asked.

The four friends took a few steps away from Ebenezer Grapefruit.

They did not comprehend how such an old fruit moved as fast as he did without them hearing him.

Ebenezer tried to reassure the four friends.

"How do you know we are going to Aisle of Cookies?" Edward asked.

Ebenezer rubbed his wrinkly chin.

"Just a lucky guess," he said.

Ebenezer started walking towards the bus stop.

"Wait! Mr. Grapefruit," Ava said.

Ebenezer stopped.

"Yes Miss Ava how can I help you."

"You clearly now something about Aisle of Cookies, I am guessing we are heading in the right direction. Am I right?"

"You may be right," Ebenezer said cryptically.

"Can you help us? Edward has gotten us here but can you suggest anything else?" Ava said with unblinking eyes.

Ebenezer laughed and slapped his knee.

"Of course I can give you some information, but like I said, you must be very careful when in the Aisle of Cookies."

The four friends cheered Ebenezer was going to help them.

"You will have to walk a long distance, but once you get to the cobblestone road, it will guide you were you want to go. I will point you in the right direction," Ebenezer said as he pointed.

"How are you so sure?" Edward asked.

"He's old. He has to know something," Zachary interjected.

Edward, Ava and Alex shook their heads at Zachary.

"What?" Zachary said.

"Excuse our friend's rudeness," Ava said.

"Have you been to the Aisle of Cookies?" Edward eyes widened with the questions.

Zachary, Ava and Alex also waited in anticipation to what Ebenezer was about to say.

"Hey a wild animal!" Ebenezer said as he pointed behind them.

The four friends turned around to see what Ebenezer had pointed at.

"Nothing there. He must be senile," Zachary said.

The four fruits turned around to talk to Ebenezer, but he was gone, vanishing into thin air.

"Where did he go? Alex asked.

The four friends looked all around but found no sign of Ebenezer Grapefruit.

"Oh fruit that's creepy," Edward said.

"You said it brother," Zachary replied.

"Do you think he was telling the truth about how to get to Aisle of Cookies?" Alex asked.

"Not sure, he was quite weird," Edward said.

"Weird is an understatement. He fell off the turnip truck," Zachary said laughing.

"Well I believe him, besides do you have an idea where to go Edward?" Ava said with her hands on her hips.

Edward shook his head.

"Not exactly," Edward said.

"Well boys start walking. Talking about it is not going to get us there," Ava said as she started walking in the direction Ebenezer had pointed to.

Edward, Zachary and Alex followed behind Ava as the hot sun beat down on them.

Chapter 4

Edward, Zachary, Ava and Alex traveled a whole day thru the hot sun and nightfall had begun to set in with a refreshing welcoming breeze.

"Edward how much longer?" Zachary cried.

Edward shrugged his shoulders. "I guess we are close,"

The cobblestone path they had been on ended in front of busted wooden boards and a pile of stones. Edward studied the wooden boards and stones.

"I think we are here!" he said, pointing in excitement.

One of the broken boards read *Aisle of Cookies*.

"This is it we are here!" Ava shouted.

"Finally," Zachary said. "My legs are getting tired and if I had to walk another…"

"Zachary shut up! You want to check this out," Alex hollered.

"Did you just tell me to shut up dufus?" Zachary said.

"Don't call me dufus. I will peel your yellow behind," Alex said.

Zachary thought about his butt being peeled by Alex. Zachary shuddered at the thought.

"Alright enough with the hostilities," Edward interjected. "What do you want to show us Alex?"

Alex picked up another piece of the board that read 'Beware! Enter at your own peril'.

Edward started to get nervous.

"I told you this was a terrible idea Zachary. I told you, I told you, I told you," Edward repeated.

"Will somebody turn him off repeat," Zachary jested. "Relax boss the four of us will be OK. Let's get excited about this. We got you Edward the obvious brains here. We have Alex the brawny one. We obviously know whom the tuff one is, and it's not you Edward," as he glanced over at Ava. "And you got me the charming, and a brave one," Zachary puffed out his chest.

The three friends laughed at Zachary.

"Yeah right charming, that's a good one and your bravery could also be called foolish at times," Edward chastised.

"Stop being jealous you all can't be as good as me," Zachary insisted.

"So are we going to do this boy's, or are we just going to stand here and bicker?" Ava quizzed.

Sensing they might have sounded silly Edward and Zachary held their heads down.

"So let's proceed with caution. The sign is our warning," she said.

Edward and Zachary looked at the pile of rocks and boards then at Alex.

"Alex your strength is needed here big guy," Edward said.

Alex did not always have much to say, but when it came to exercise he let his body do the talking.

"All right guys and Ava give me some room," Alex instructed.

Alex bent down and started picking up the boards and heavy stones. As his arm muscles bulged, he quickly cleared the boards and stones without breaking a sweat.

"Okay guys. I'm done," Alex said.

A hole had been hidden by the debris. They stared at each other in dismay.

"I guess this is the way to the Aisle of Cookies," Edward declared.

"Yeah fruits let's do this!" Zachary shouted.

Before anyone could say anything, Zachary jumped into the tunnel.

Edward shook his head. "Well guys let's go in," Edward carefully walked in.

Ava and Alex followed behind. The tunnel lit up with torches on the walls.

"Maybe we should grab some of these torches in case the tunnel runs out of them," Edward cautioned.

"Good thinking," Ava said to Edward.

They grabbed the torches off the walls and proceeded down the narrow tunnel. The tunnel narrowed as they walked one by one behind each other. Zachary led the way with Edward, Ava and Alex following behind.

The walls crawled with slimy green moss as the light of the torches illuminated them.

"Boo! Boo! Boo!" Zachary said trying to imitate a ghost.

Zachary voice echoed throughout the tunnel.

"Cut it out!" Edward screeched.

"Am I going to wake up the bread," Zachary replied.

Alex and Ava laughed at Zachary's comments. Edward elbowed Zachary in the back. Zachary moaned as he rubbed his back.

They had been walking through the winding tunnel for twenty minutes, when they came upon a large open cavern. The roof of the cavern had stalactite hanging from them.

"This looks like the end of the tunnel," Ava observed.

The four of them scanned the cavern. Several cave drawings had been painted on the wall and floor.

"We came this far and now we are stuck at a dead end," Zachary howled.

"Great idea," Alex barked at Zachary.

Zachary and Alex began to argue with each other, when Ava walked over to Edward. Edward lost in his thought studied the paintings.

"Edward what is it?" Ava asked.

Edward smiled, "We are not stuck. This is not a dead end. Ava see the drawings on the wall and on the floor?"

"Yes," she replied.

"I believe the drawings are a puzzle and the right solution should open another passage way for us."

Alex and Zachary stopped arguing and walked over to where Ava and Edward were standing.

"What's this you say?" Zachary asked.

"While you guys were bickering I realized these paintings are a puzzle and the solution of the puzzle should open another passageway."

Zachary leaned on Edward. "So what's the solution Edison?"

Edwards pushed Zachary out of his way and walked towards the wall. On the wall the panels had drawings on them. Edward then glanced at the ground and studied the panels.

"Give me a moment and let me think. There may be booby-traps here," Edward cautioned.

Zachary, Alex, and Ava eyed each other. The three of them stepped away from the panels on the floor.

Edward continued to study the paintings on the wall. On the first panel a drawing of a cake. On the second panel a drawing of French Fries and on the last panel a drawing of salad.

On the floor the first panel had a drawing of a soda can, the center panel had a drawing of a glass of milk, and the last panel had a drawing of a glass of water.

"So which panels do we start hitting?" Zachary impatiently asked.

"I think you press the water, milk and salad," Alex reasoned.

"That sounds stupid," Zachary snapped.

"Now boys let's give Edward some quiet time so he can think," Ava instructed.

"Thanks," Edward said.

Edward's mouth widened into a grin. "Guys I think I found the solution."

"I hope so, because If you don't I won't let you hear the end of it," Zachary joked.

Edward smiled, "I hope so to because I sure don't want to hear your big mouth."

Edward began to explain the solution.

"Alex I am not sure why you picked those panels."

Alex leaned closer to Edward. "Because I am right, am I right?"

Zachary scoffed. "You right! That's funny. When rivers of juice freeze over."

Edward continued. "No, you are not right. Each panel on the wall corresponds with a panel on the floor. So I matched water to salad and soda to the French Fries and milk matched with cake."

Ava's eyes widened. "I understand now," she said.

"Well I don't. Edward how about you clue me in," Zachary demanded.

"All right don't get your peel in a bunch. I came up with milk and cake that is the closest thing to cookies and milk, which go well together. I figured the other drawings followed a similar pattern."

The three of them nodded their heads in approval.

"What if you are wrong?" Alex asked.

"Let's just hope I am not. Remember the potential boo-by traps."

Their spirits deflated again.

Zachary moaned. "You had to say the booby trap word again."

Edward walked over to the milk panel. He was about to step on the panel when a thought occurred to him.

"I forgot guys besides picking the right panels we have to be correct on the sequence of panels to press."

"Was it milk before cake or cake before milk?" Edward said out loud. "Milk can wash down the cake that you eat. So cake panel first then milk panel second," he beamed with confidence.

Edward walked over to the right side of the wall and pressed the cake panel. The ground began to rumble and shake for a brief moment before the cavern became still again.

Edward walked over and stepped on the center panel of the milk drawing. The cavern began to shake, and the ground began to move. The four of them held onto each other as they started to sink into the ground.

"I thought you got it right!" Zachary yelled at Edward. "Some kind of genius you are, now we are going to end up bread, thanks for nothing!"

They began sinking further into the ground. The dirt was coming perilously close to cover them, when all of sudden they stopped sinking.

The four of them stared at each other in disbelief.

"Whew! Zachary said. "That was close."

The earth suddenly opened up, and they fell thru and into a long wet hole. They slid down the tube screaming all the way down. They slid down the hole before being rudely dumped out into shallow water.

Ava stood up in the water. "Where are we Edward?"

Edward turned around to see where they were dumped from.

"Wait a minute, is this some kind of marsh?" Edward said as he took a step back, "I don't think we are in Molasses anymore," he said pointing to a large dark mountain.

Their mouths dropped in awe.

Ava gasped. "Is that what I think it is?"

Edwards's heart raced. "If you are thinking that the mountain looks like chocolate I would say your right."

Alex jumped in the conversation.

"That would mean we are in the..."

Zachary cut Alex off in mid-sentence.

"The Aisle of Cookies!"

They all jumped up with a cheer and hugged each other.

"So what's next?" Alex asked.

The three of them turned to Edward.

"Well the first thing to do is get out of this water, and head toward those trees," he pointed. "Hopefully we can get some sort of direction of where to go."

Chapter 5

The four of them trekked thru the marshy waters. They noticed a black cloud moving towards them.

"What is that?" Ava said pointing towards the invading black cloud.

"Probably nothing but a rain cloud," Zachary said.

"That's not a rain cloud Mr. Brain," Alex said to Zachary.

"Like you would know." Zachary snapped.

A buzzing black cloud edged closer to them.

"Is the buzzing sound coming from the cloud?" Edward asked as he tried to determine the direction of the sound.

"Yes I guess so, and we should hurry. We need to get to dry land," Alex urged.

"Why?" Zachary said in a mocking voice.

"The cloud is a swarm of fruit flies!" Alex shouted.

The cloud of insects edged closer to them.

"He is right!" Edward shrieked. "Run!"

They scrambled thru the water as the fruit flies began to descend on them. Zachary turned around as they raced toward land. "These are not your average blood sucking fruit flies. Man, they are enormous!"

They swatted at the swarm of insects above their heads. When they reached land the fruit flies retreated back over the swamp. The black cloud and the high pitch buzzing disappeared in the distance.

The four of them bent over with hands on knees as they tried to catch their breath.

"This is looking like a bad idea Zachary," Edward said as he nervously looked around for other dangers.

As prideful as Zachary was he had to agree with Edward's assessment.

"You may be right my fruit. Sounded like a brilliant idea didn't it guys?" Zachary asked trying to get some kind of support from them.

"A good idea, but maybe it's time to head back," Ava said.

"We can't go the way we came unless you want another close encounter of the fruit fly kind?" Alex said.

"Yeah you're right, but what's are options?" Ava asked.

"Well apparently not many since we don't have a way back," Edward said.

"What are you saying my well rounded friend?" Zachary asked.

"See for yourself," Edwards said as he pointed in the direction of the swamp.

The hole they had slid down was gone, only a mountain remained.

"Where did the hole we slid down go? It was there a moment ago," Zachary said.

Alex began to panic. "We are trapped here," he said.

Edward stood still thinking.

"How can you just stand by and do nothing?" Zachary shouted at Edward.

Edward thought for a moment before he addressed his friends. "I remembered the stories about Aisle of Cookies. I thought the stories were make believe, but this place is real. I have no doubt we are in the Aisle of Cookies," Edward said as he looked at each of them in the eye.

Edward continued.

"We have heard tales of fruits coming back from the Aisle of Cookies, usually from the older fruits. We thought they were crazy, but there has to be some truth to their stories, and don't forget Ebenezer Grapefruit. He must have been to the Aisle of Cookies. Don't you agree?"

Ava, Alex and Zachary nodded their heads in agreement.

Edward continued. "If their stories are true then we have a chance to go home. We must believe. We came here for an adventure and an adventure is what we shall have," he said.

The three of them cheered Edward. Their confidence grew.

"That was a great speech," Ava said to Edward.

"I didn't know you had the seeds in you," Zachary said as he gave a congratulatory slap on his best friend's back.

Alex picked Edward up and gave him a big hug.

Chapter 6

"So let's go," Zachary said as he led the way into the forests.

A bright blue light flashed as each of them entered the forest.

"What was that bright light?" Ava asked.

Edward was about to answer when he got hit in the head with an object.

"Hey?" As he rubbed his head.

Another object hit him in the head again.

"What the heck."

Edward stopped in mid-sentence and spotted Zachary picking some objects of the ground.

"Zachary what are you doing?"

Zachary had a sly grin on his face. Zachary then threw another object at Edward hitting him on the head.

Are you crazy fruit?" Edward yelled.

"He clearly is crazy," Alex chimed in.

"You almost put one my eyes out with those rocks," Edward said.

"Those aren't rocks I am throwing at you," Zachary replied.

"If they are not rocks what are they?" Edward asked.

Zachary went into a wind up and threw another object at Edward.

This time Edward ducked. As the object went past Edward's head a bright blue light flashed behind him.

"I think that answers your question Ava on what's causing the blue light," Alex said.

Edward walked towards Alex. "Amazing. Guys come here," Edward instructed.

Zachary and Ava walked towards Edward and Alex.

"Stretch your hands out," Edward instructed.

They did as Edward instructed, and touched an invisible energy field.

"We activated the energy field when we entered the forest," Edward said.

Zachary picked up one of the objects, put it into his mouth, and started chewing.

"Fruit I am going to love this place," Zachary said with a dark toothy grin.

Edward, Ava and Alex scrunched up their faces in disgust.

"Eww!" Ava said.

"What are you doing eating rubbish stupid?" Alex said.

"Didn't we come to a decision on who the stupid one was, and it was obviously you, besides fruit genius this is not rubbish its chocolate chips. Look around you. Boy you guys are not observant," Zachary said as he bent down, and grabbed a handful of chocolate chips. "Try some," he said as he handed them the rock sized chocolate chips.

Ava, Edward and Alex hesitantly took a chocolate chip.

Edward sniffed the rock sized chip and smiled.

"I believe you are right Zachary."

"Are you going to sniff or eat the chips silly?" Zachary replied.

Edward put the chocolate chip in his mouth and slowly began to eat. The gooey chips stuck to his teeth. "Umm this is good. I didn't know this would be yummy," Edward said as he licked the chocolate off his lips.

Ava and Alex also tried some of the rock sized chocolate chips.

Ava and Alex also had gooey smiles of chocolate.

"Look around Edward a lot of the forest is made of sweets. I just wanted to remind you guys this was my idea to come here." Zachary bragged.

The aroma of candy and chocolate filled the air.

"Well we can't stand here forever we need to move on," Ava said.

"Speak for yourself Ava," Zachary said as he ate another chocolate chip. "I could stay here forever," he said with his mouth full.

"I agree with Ava," Alex said. "We need to go. Remember our goal is to find a way out of here."

Edward agreed. "Let's go Zachary," Edward said.

"Who knows what else we can find in the Aisle of Cookies, but we won't know by standing here eating chocolate chips," Ava said.

"All right, all right, let's go," Zachary said.

Edward gazed up into the trees. "Do you guys know what time it is? Hard to tell how long we have been on this trip. I think the time has changed since we entered the forest."

They glanced up in the trees to see how much light showed. The tall trees seemed to block out most of the sunlight.

"Hard to tell what time it is. We may have four hours of daylight or fewer," Alex said.

"Well if the shade down here starts to get darker this will be are clue night is approaching, and I sure don't want to be stuck out here in the middle of the night," Edward said.

"You can say that again my fruit," Zachary said.

They started walking thru the heavy brush, occasionally looking up into the trees trying to determine the daylight situation. After a half an hour of walking thru the dense foliage of peppermint leafs, Ava abruptly stopped.

"Do you hear that?" She asked.

"Hear what?" Edward asked.

"That sound, sounds like running water," she said.

"I hear it," Zachary said.

"So do I," Alex added.

A pathway carved out of the forest in front of them. Edward noticed the subtle rumbling sound of water.

"I think the sound is coming straight and to the left," Ava said.

Ava walked towards the rumbling sound, the three young fruits followed behind her.

Ava brushed the thick peppermint leaves away from her as she drew closer to the sound. The three boys tried to keep up with her.

Ava stopped. She came to the edge of the forest. Ava raised her hand to warn the boys.

"What is it Ava?" Edward asked.

"Be careful," she said pointing down.

At the edge of the forest, the ground descended several feet into a vast chasm that had a white liquid substance running thru it. The roar of the white liquid echoed off the chasm walls.

"Let's go check it out," Zachary said.

The rest of them agreed with Zachary and carefully climbed down the steep embankment. As they climbed down the rocky chasm walls, Alex slipped dislodging a rock which fell on Edwards head. The blow from the rock knocked Edward off the wall sending him tumbling down the chasm wall onto the black sands, on the bank of the white liquid river.

Zachary, Ava and Alex rushed down the wall to Edwards's side. Edward was knocked out by the fall as he lay on the black sand.

Edward slowly awoke to Ava, Zachary and Alex standing over him with worried faces.

"You okay Bro? You had a nasty fall," Zachary said.

Edward held his head. "What happened?" Edward asked.

Zachary answered. "Well Oinks Mc-klutz here,"

pointing at Alex, "slipped knocking out a rock which bonked you on the head."

"Sorry about that. It was an accident," Alex said, sheepishly shrugging his shoulders.

"No worries," Edward replied.

Ava examined Edwards head. "You have a slight bruise on your head. You should be all right," she said.

Edward tried to pull himself up, but his knees were wobbly. The three of them grabbed Edward and steadied him.

They had temporarily forgotten why they had come down the chasm, when the roar of the white liquid grabbed their attention.

Chapter 7

Zachary ran towards the river's edge kicking up the black sand. Edward looked at Ava and Alex and shook his head.

"Let's go follow that piñata," Edward said.

Zachary dipped his hands in the white liquid and began to drink.

"Are you crazy?" Edward yelled.

"Why yes I am," Zachary said laughing at Edward.

Zachary again tasted the white liquid and smiled. "Can you believe this is a river of milk? Come on guys take a drink," Zachary begged.

Edward, Alex and Ava all took a sip from the milky river.

"This is tasty, and good for the bones," Alex said.

"I guess not all of Aisle of Cookies can be bad for you," Ava said.

Zachary bent down to tie his sneakers when his eyes bulged with excitement. "As I suspected crushed Oreo's," he said reaching down and putting the black sand in his mouth. Zachary licked the crushed Oreo sand from his lips.

"You're out of control," Edward said.

"How do you know so much about sweets?" Ava asked.

"He is a connoisseur of unhealthy food," Edward said.

"I believe that. Look at him all soft and mushy," Alex said.

"Hey guys I am right here you know," Zachary said annoyed with their criticism of him.

"Now what do we do?" Alex asked.

"Well I think we should go swimming in the river of milk," Zachary said as he raced thru the Oreo cookie sand, and then dove into the milky river.

Zachary waived to them come in. "Guys what's an adventure without having some fun?" He said.

"Zach's right. We did not come here to work but to explore," Ava said.

Ava ran and giggled as she jumped in the river of milky goodness.

"I don't know," said Edward nervously.

"Live it up a little, dude," Alex said slapping Edward on the back as he made his way down to the river.

Edward sighed. "They are right," he said to himself. "I am coming guys," he said while running thru the Oreo sand.

Edward tripped over his feet and rolled down the sandy shore. When he stood up bits of cookie sand covered him.

Hey clumsy! With all that Oreo on you, you look good enough to eat," Zachary said as he licked his lips.

Ava and Alex laughed.

Edward walked casually to the edge of the river near Zachary. Edward did a cannonball and splashed Zachary knocking him over with a wave of milk.

They all laughed and played in the river. Edward jumped on Zachary shoulders, and Ava jumped on Alex's shoulder as they wrestled with each other.

"You're going down," Ava said grinning at Edward.

"Not before you do," Edward said as their arms locked together.

Ava and Alex were able to topple over Edward and Zachary into the milk.

"This is fabulous," Ava said as she splashed around in the milk.

As the four of them continued to goof around, they did

not realize the milky river had been steadily rising. As the river rose the Oreo cookie shore began to disappear.

Edward realized that something was wrong.

"Guys I can't touch the bottom anymore," he said as he began to tread milk.

"Me either," Alex and Ava said in unison.

The only one who still touched the bottom was Zachary, and he would be treading milk frightfully soon.

"The sand!" Zachary pointed.

The beach was almost gone.

"The milk is rising guys. We have to swim back to the beach," Edward said.

They swam for the beach, but the shoreline became smaller and smaller as the milky river steadily rose until no more sand was left. The milky river turned a chocolate flavored color from the mixing of milk and the Oreo sand.

Zachary eyed the now flowing chocolate milk. *Under other circumstances this would be fantastic,* Zachary thought.

"Guys let's wait to the river gets high enough, and we can make it back to ledge we came down from," Edward said.

As soon as Edward spoke they felt themselves move rapidly downstream.

"This is not good!" Zachary yelled.

The momentum of the river took them further downstream.

"Guys reach out your hands and try to hold on to each other!" Alex screamed his voice barely audible over the roar of the raging river.

Zachary and Ava were able to get to Alex, but Edward was drifting further and further away from them. They screamed in unison for Edward.

"Come on buddy! Swim! Swim!" Zachary yelled.

Edward was a poor swimmer. The milky river splashed in his face, causing him to be disoriented.

Don't panic, he thought.

He started swimming in the direction of his friends voices, pushing his arms and legs as hard and as fast as they could go. Edward was getting tired, and he was losing hope he would make it, when he felt a hand grab his arm.

"I got you buddy," Zachary said.

The milk cleared from Edwards eyes. He saw Zachary, Ava and Alex.

"You need to go to the gym. Do you call that swimming?" Zachary teased.

Zachary hid his feelings from them. He was terribly worried he almost lost his best friend.

Edward was relieved he had made it to his friends. The river continued to take them downstream.

"Thanks Zachary for saving me," Edward said.

"No problem. You don't have to thank me," Zachary said trying not to sound mushy.

"Good to have you back," Ava said to Edward.

"Thanks," Edward said, partially out of breath.

"So where do you think this is going to take us?" Alex asked the group.

The milky river became calm as they continued downstream.

"Whew! I thought the river was going to swallow us up," Edward said.

"It sure almost got you," Zachary said with a wink to Edward.

"Whatever," Edward said.

As they drifted down the river, the rocky ridges and the outline of tall trees surrounded them.

Zachary moaned. "No way out of this milky mess. Even if we swim towards the trees we can't climb those jagged rocks," he said.

Edward pointed further down the river. "I don't think it's going to matter anyway," he said.

Edward spotted several branches of trees in the river disappear from view.

"Oh fruit that can't be what I think it is," Zachary said.

"You've got to be kidding just when I thought it could not get any worse," Alex said.

"What are we going to do Edward? We are getting closer to the edge of the milky-fall!" Ava yelled.

"Not much we can do. We are stuck between a rock and a hard place. We are going to have to ride the milky-fall down," Edward said.

"Fruit you are crazy. Have you lost a few seeds?" Zachary asked. "We don't know how far we will fall or if there are jagged rocks below which will smash our poor little fruit bodies to pieces?"

"True all that can happen or we make it out alive but we have no other options," Edward said.

They knew Edward was right. There was not enough time to swim to the edge of the river, and make the perilous climb up the canyon walls.

"Nice knowing you," Zachary said sarcastically.

The sound of the milky-fall grew louder and louder as they drew closer and closer to its edge, a piece of wood drifted close to them.

"Grab the wood, maybe we can ride it down!" Zachary hollered.

They clung to the piece of drift wood right before they went down the milky-fall. They rode the log of wood screaming all the way down the milky-fall. They did not fall far as they splashed into the milky lagoon.

"I am alive! We made it!" Zachary said jubilantly as he hugged each of them. "I did not doubt it for a second."

"Yeah right," Edward replied.

They were all relieved they had survived the milky-fall.

"Let's get out of this milky mess and head towards the beach," Ava said pointing to the sparkling beach in front of them.

"Good idea," Edward said.

"Maybe those sparkles in the sand are jewels, like diamonds or something," Zachary said excitedly.

The four of them swam towards the sparkling beach. When they stepped out of the milky lagoon, the sparkles of beach were gone.

"Must have been the way the sun rays were hitting the sand," Edward said.

"Sand? I don't think its sand. I bet you it's some sort of cookie," Zachary suggested.

"No, I think its sand," Edward replied.

"Horseradish," Zachary said as he bent over and scooped

the sand up and put it in his mouth. "Eww!" Zachary said, spitting the sand out.

Zachary continued to exaggerate spitting sand from his mouth.

"Zachary get serious. We have to find our way back home," Edward said.

"Right you are," Alex replied.

The four of them walked through the beach and over a sand dune. They had walked for several minutes when Ava spotted a small village.

"I can't believe it. A village here?" she said.

Chapter 8

The four of them walked towards the village.

"This is unbelievable. This is our chance to find signs of life," Edward said as he began to walk faster towards the village.

"Hey slow down. Let's not throw caution to the wind," Ava said to Edward.

They followed a path made out of ginger bread bricks. They could see large snowcapped mountains not far from the village.

"The mountains are beautiful," Ava said as she admired the scenic view.

"Yeah they sure are. I bet those snowcapped mountains aren't snow, but vanilla ice cream and the base of the mountain are large cones," Zachary said as he licked his lips in delight.

They all looked at the snow-capped mountains.

"You might be right about the ice cream mountain top," Alex said.

"I wonder if the mountains are ice cream cones." Edward pondered.

They continued down the ginger bread road and entered the village. Several homes with straw rooftops made of licorice lay in a circle. In the middle of the circle was a large fountain of milk. Small cookie children played in the fountain of milk.

"Those children are about our age," Zachary said.

The four of them were excited to find life, but they may have been too excited. The sound of their raised voices and strange appearance scared the children. The children ran off into their houses.

"Why are they running from us?" Alex asked.

"They probably got a glimpse of that large head of yours," Zachary said to Alex.

Edward ignored Zachary and Alex. He waved to the fleeing cookie children.

"Come back here. We come in peace," Edward said.

"Edward you make us sound like aliens," Zachary said.

"Maybe we are to them Zachary. We are different from them," Ava said.

"I think we may have problem," Edward said pointing.

The older cookies of the village came out of their homes carrying sticks made out of cinnamon. They approached the four of them angrily shouting and waving their sticks in the air.

"This can't be good," Zachary said.

"Who are you? And what are you doing here?" The elder cookie with long white hair and pointy beard demanded.

Zachary began to approach him confidently, and was about to speak before Edward stopped him.

"Diplomacy my fruit, let me handle this," Edward said as he approached the elderly cookie.

"We are from the town of Safe and Fresh, and we came in search of the Aisle of Cookies."

The elder cookie eyed Edward and his friends. He rubbed his beard in deep thought.

"We are friendly," Edward added.

Ava, Zachary and Alex nodded their heads in agreement.

"Can you have your cookies put down their sticks?" Edward asked.

The elder cookie motioned to his people to put down

their weapons. The village cookies obeyed the elder and lowered their sticks.

"So you are fruits from the other side?" The elder cookie asked.

The four of them nodded in agreement.

"We are aware of fruits and others from Botany County. It is not often we get visitors from the other side," the elder said. "You are healthy like us. You must be friends."

The four friends were surprised the elder new of Botany County.

Zachary couldn't help himself as he blurted out, "Healthy you obviously don't know you are cookies."

"Zachary! Let's be polite," Ava said.

"That's okay you are new to our land. Zachary we are healthy cookies. No sugar and made up of natural preservatives."

Zachary shook his head in disagreement. Zachary then turned to Edward.

"Is he speaking a foreign language?" Zachary asked.

"No, he is not," Edward said impatiently.

"What Edward?" Zachary asked.

Edward ignored Zachary and turned to the elder cookie.

"Sorry for my friend he is not so bright," Edward said.

"Hey!" Zachary protested.

Edward continued talking to the elder cookie.

"I did not realize the Aisle of Cookies actually had healthy ones residing in it."

"Oh yes there are lots of healthy things here, but we live in constant fear of one particular unhealthy overlord who took over the Aisle of Cookies. We try to stay away from those horrible cookies and mind our own business. This new ruler does not like anything healthy which makes me wonder why you are here. You are in grave danger by being here."

"Danger?" Ava asked nervously.

"Yes. You will need to leave here as soon as possible before they find you."

"Who will come and find us?" Alex asked.

"King Nutty and his army of chocolate chips and fudge," the elder replied.

"Sounds delicious," Zachary said.

Edward elbowed Zachary.

"King Nutty what kind of cookie is he?" Zachary asked.

One of the older male cookies came forward.

"King Nutty is a peanut butter cookie. He has many under his power. He is quite…"

"Let me guess. He is crazy," Zachary interrupted.

Zachary started laughing at his own joke.

Everyone around him was not amused.

"Guys get it King Nutty and crazy," Zachary said laughing at himself again.

Zachary looked at the serious faces around and stopped laughing.

"You guys are a bunch of sour grapes."

The elder cookie put his hand on his long gray beard. "I don't want to sound rude because you all are a guest in our village, but you can only stay the night. After your stay, we will send you in the right direction to get you back home."

"Thank you for letting us stay the night," Ava said.

"Some kind of hospitality," Zachary mumbled.

Edward and Alex also thanked the elder and the other village cookies.

"Well, while you are here lets us celebrate," the elder said.

"Celebrate what," Zachary said with an attitude.

"Our new friendship," the elder said.

"You have a funny way of being friendly," Zachary said as he eyed the elder cookie.

"Easy my friend," the elder said.

"There he goes with friend again," Zachary said.

"Let us dance and have a bountiful dinner," said the elder.

"Dinner! Oh, you are going to feed us. Why didn't you say that before? Friend," Zachary said as he gave the elder a hug.

Edward and Alex grabbed Zachary off the elder.

"I can't wait to eat. I bet they got some yummy food. I'm starving!"

Zachary screamed.

"You are always hungry I can't believe you're not fat," Edward said.

"I am hungry too," Alex said.

"Well its settled come with us," the elder said as he motioned them to follow him.

The crowd of village cookies parted as Edward, Zachary, Ava and Alex followed the elder into the heart of the village.

The elder called out in a loud voice. He raised up his arms. "Cookies of Natural Way we have visitors from a distant land. Let us show them are hospitality," he said.

The elder and the other cookies led the four fruits to a banquet hall.

Chapter 9

On the stage in front of them, a band played polka music.

As they sat at the table a bunch of cookies came out with trays of food.

"Oh yeah," Zachary said with a smile as he pounded his fork and knife on the table.

"Show some manners Zachary," Ava scolded.

Zachary relaxed and put the fork and knife down, but he was still excited at the various trays of food being placed on their table.

Several plates of unidentifiable food were made and placed in front of them.

"Eat my friends," said the elder.

Zachary looked at Edward and said in a low voice, "Do you know what this stuff is?"

Edward stared at his plate of food and shook his head. Edward turned to Ava and Alex.

"Do you guys know what this is?"

Ava shook her head, but Alex stared at his plate.

"It looks familiar. I can't put my finger on it," Alex said.

Not wanting to appear rude Edward decided to take a bite instead of asking what was on his plate. He stuck his fork into his light colored square shape meal. As he moved the fork with the mystery food towards his mouth Zachary, Alex and Ava watched closely.

He scrunched up his face as he swallowed.

"What is it?" Zachary asked.

Edward shrugged his shoulders. "I don't know, but it's not good," Edward said in a low voice so the elder and other cookies could not overhear him.

Zachary not caring blurted to the elder.

"What is that?" Pointing rudely to Edwards's plate.

The elder smiled. "Tofu," he said.

"Toe what?" Zachary said confused.

"That's what it is. I like tofu!" Alex exclaimed.

Zachary pushed his plate away. "Okay I am ready for dessert," he said.

"You must eat dinner first," the elder said.

Edward, Zachary, and Ava eyed their plates with apprehension while Alex had already started eating.

"This is great," Alex said with tofu and lettuce flying out of his mouth.

"And you said I don't have manners," Zachary said nudging Edward to take a look at Alex.

Edward, Ava and Zachary grudgingly ate their tofu salad.

After several minutes of eating, they were done.

Alex had extra-large helpings, in addition to his first plate. Alex waited for the other three to finish.

"Okay now can we get to the dessert?" Zachary asked.

"Sure bring out the ice cream," the elder ordered.

"Ice cream now that's what I am talking about," Zachary said.

The four of them wiggled in their chairs with delight as they waited for their ice cream to come out.

A large bowl of vanilla ice cream was carried out on a tray held by two cookies.

"Wow! That is one mountain of ice cream!" Edward shouted.

Surprised by Edwards reaction his three friends began to laugh.

"What?" Edward asked.

"Oh nothing, funny to see you so excited," Ava said.

Edward became embarrassed.

"Is that fudge on top of the ice cream?" Zachary said pointing to the fudge cap on their mountain of ice cream.

"You bet it is! Edward said with a big grin.

"Calm down their chief you may lose a seed," Zachary teased.

"Shut up," Edward said not taking his eyes off the delicious looking ice cream.

The cookie servers began to dish the ice cream starting with Alex, followed by Ava.

"Umm this is tasty, not like any vanilla ice cream I have had before," Alex said.

Ava took a spoonful of her ice cream. "Delicious. What are the black dots in the ice cream?" Ava asked one of the servers.

"Those are vanilla beans. You're eating all-natural vanilla ice cream," the server said.

The server dished Edward who tasted the ice cream with a broad smile. As the server was about to dish Zachary his ice cream, several villagers ran into the hall.

"They are here!" They exclaimed.

"Who is here?" The elder asked.

"King Nutty and his soldiers! They draw near, sir!" The village cookies exclaimed.

Edward spit out his ice cream when he heard the name King Nutty. Tension began to grow in the hall. The servers with haste took the large bowl of ice cream away.

"No! I want my ice cream. Where are you going?" Zachary bellowed.

Zachary's arms stretched out beckoning the ice cream to return.

"You must have been spotted. We must take you guys out of here," the elder said.

The sound of King Nutty's and his soldier's footstep vibrated throughout the hall. Parents held their scared children.

A village cookie spoke rapidly to the elder. "Sir they should be at the outer perimeter of the village. It won't be long," he said.

"Okay let's get some hands over here to block this door. This should give us some time to get our guest out."

Some of the stronger cookies lined up and leaned against the door.

"Let's leave out the back door," the elder said pointing to a red door at the back of the hall.

Chapter 10

As the four of them ran towards the backdoor, loud thuds came from the main door.

"Are they after us? Edward nervously asked.

"They are?" The elder replied.

"What do they want from us? Edward asked.

"Who cares let's get out of here," Zachary said.

"We can't hold the door much longer!" a villager screamed.

The door the men had been holding burst open knocking them off their feet. From the splintered doors emerged some chocolate chip soldiers and fudge guards.

"I don't know if I should be scared or happy to see them," Zachary said as he eyed the chocolate chips on the cookies.

The elder opened the back door. "Let's go my friends," he said.

The four of them followed the elder outside.

"I am sorry friends your stay was short, but I am glad we got to meet. Follow the path ahead. The path will eventually split. Take the path to the left. Once you get back to the marsh you should be able to recognize your way home."

The four friends thanked the elder before running down the ginger bread covered road.

King Nutty's soldiers burst out of the hall and grabbed the elder.

The elder waved to them frantically. "Remember to stay away from the whirlpools," he said.

"Did you catch what he said?" Edward asked.

"Nope. I was focusing on those delicious cookies," Zachary said.

Edward shook his head at Zachary. "Did either of you hear what the elder said?" Edward asked Ava and Alex.

"No," they answered.

"Get them!" Yelled a peanut shaped cookie that had a gold crown on his head.

"I suggest we run!" yelled Ava.

The four of them ran down the path as King Nutty's soldiers gave chase.

"Guy's they are getting close!" Edward screamed.

The chocolate chip and fudge army gained on them.

"There's the fork in the road," Alex pointed to the split in the road.

"Which way did the elder say to go?" Zachary asked.

"To the left," Edwards said out of breath.

As they neared the fork in the road, two soldiers came from behind a large ginger bread tree.

"We have been ambushed," said Alex.

"We have nowhere to go," Ava said as the soldiers from the rear approached.

The soldiers then encircled the four of them.

"What do we do now?" Alex asked Edward.

Before Edward answered, a large net was thrown over them.

"Hey let us go!" The four of them shouted at their captors.

The soldiers began to back away.

"That's right you heard us. Keep on backing up," Zachary said.

Zachary did not realize the soldiers were not backing away because of him but were backing away out of respect for their king.

"All hail King Nutty!" The soldiers shouted.

King Nutty in his overweight peanut shaped body

slowly approached. His small cold eyes stared at the four friends underneath the net.

"So these are the intruders into my land," he said looking at them in disgust. "I can't stand healthy things. So why did you come to my land? Did you come to infect my wickedly wonderful world of sugar, sweats and all things unhealthy?"

"Answer the king," one of the soldiers said as he jabbed them with his staff.

Zachary kept looking at all the delicious cookies surrounding him. "You sound crazy, but you look very tasty," he said with wide eyes at the king.

"Oh fruit," Edward said shaking his head.

"What did you say?" The king demanded.

"He did not say anything. I mean he did not mean anything," Edward said trying to cover up Zachary's foot in mouth remark.

Zachary ignored the king's demand to answer him and turned to his buddy Edward. "Man this stinks we came here to eat sweets and now we get captured by them."

Edward shook his head in amazement at his best friend's ability to say the wrong things at the wrong time.

Chapter 11

The four of them were whisked off in a cart with strong bamboo poles so they could not escape. The cart with the four trapped friend's raced towards King Nutty's castle. Ava had taken notice what direction they were going while Edward, Alex and Zachary discussed their fate.

Occasionally the soldiers would tell them to shut up. After a short ride over rolling hills and through a valley, they came to a stop at a bridge. A hundred feet below them were jagged rocks. On the other side of the bridge dark, gloomy clouds patrolled the sky.

King Nutty was the first to cross the bridge as his soldiers carried him on his throne across the heavily built wooden bridge.

The four friends were surprised at the contrast of the beautiful Aisle of Cookies they had entered, and the scary one in front of them.

"I don't want be here anymore," Edward said as they moved along the bridge.

"I hope we don't fall," Alex said as he learned against the bamboo bars.

"A fall would not bode well for my soft beautiful yellow skin," Zachary said.

As the cart moved closer to the other side of the bridge, they noticed a rotten land. The rotten area gave off a pungent odor.

Zachary was the first to comment on the odor. "Edward this place stinks like your rear end."

"Zachary this is no time for jokes. Can't you see we are in trouble?" Edward said.

"Who's joking? Your butt stinks," Zachary responded.

As Zachary and Edward squabbled, Ava and Alex were trying to get their attention. "Hey guys," as they both nudged Edward and Zachary.

Ava and Alex pointed to a large castle with a flag of King Nutty on top. The castle was surrounded by a moat of spoiled milk. A draw bridge lowered down so they could enter the castle.

"Wow!" Zachary said.

"It looks quite dirty," Ava said.

"This is really bad guys," Edward said.

"We need to stay positive," Alex said.

King Nutty glared at the prisoners.

"Lock them in the prison. You will face your fate in the morning," he said as he glared at them.

"Yeah right stay positive," Zachary said to Alex.

The large gate to the castle opened. The soldiers carted the four friends into the castle. The castle was lit with several torches.

The soldiers laughed and taunted them as they pulled them further into the castle. Several soldiers stood guard throughout the castle. They were each carrying long stick weapons. They had menacing faces as they eyed the captured fruits.

The guard led the four friends to a wooden door. The guard gave three loud knocks on the door. A panel on the door slide open and two eyes peered out.

"What?" A loud angry voice said from the other side of the door.

"We have four new prisoners," the soldier said.

The door creaked opened, and a prison guard pushed the four friends in.

"Welcome. I believe you will find King Nutty's accommodations to be the finest in the land," the toothless guard laughed.

The guard took the four friends down a winding staircase lit with torches. At the bottom of the staircase were several rows of prison cells. The guard spoke to another guard quietly in his ear. The second guard took the four friends to a filthy prison cell.

"Here you go. I hope you find your new home enjoyable," the guard laughed again as he locked the prison gate.

The guard walked down the hallway and stood next to another guard. Several other prisoners could be heard in the adjacent cells to the four friends.

Edward nervously eyed the prison bars. "What are we going to do? I don't want to become apple pie. I and you guys don't want to peach cobbler, banana split or orange marmalade," he said.

"Whoa Edward you are not helping the situation," Ava said.

"So what do you suggest because come tomorrow we may become what Edward said," Zachary said to Ava.

"We only have one choice," Ava said.

"What?" Alex asked.

Ava eyed her friends. "We have to escape," she said.

"Yeah right, did you fall off the turnip truck," Zachary chided.

Ava continued. "Zachary are you done acting silly? What happened to the brave banana? Did he leave and I am just looking at a mushy banana who lost his peel?"

"So you think I am brave?" Zachary said with a big grin.

"You are all brave," she said.

"Oh, you mean all of us except Edward?" Zachary said as he nudged Edward.

"Wait a minute, I can be brave," Edward insisted.

"Guys, let's focus on getting out of here. You know what morning brings," Ava said.

They all shook their heads acknowledging what their fate held.

"So what do you suggest? We are trapped in a cell underground in a large castle with guards and soldiers…" Edward paused to catch his breath, "and if, by some miracle, we do escape, I don't remember how to get back to the village."

Ava smiled at Edward. "I remember how to get back to the village."

"You sound pretty confident we are getting out of here," Alex said to Ava.

"I am sure we can get out of here. The alternative does not sound pleasant, does it?" She replied.

"This is true Ava. So, do you have a plan?" Alex asked.

Ava looked over at Edward. "Let's ask our genius Edward," Ava said with a smile.

Edward stared at Ava in disbelief. She had put him on the spot.

"Me? Why me?" He moaned.

Ava patted Edward on his shoulder. "Because you are awesome at making plans and besides we are all here to help you. I just want to let you know we all believe in you. You did figure out how to get to the Aisle of Cookie, didn't you? Remember solving the puzzle in the cave?"

Edward smiled nervously.

"She's right, my friend. You are the brains, look at the size of your head," Zachary said. "Just kidding, I am with Ava. You can do this."

"I agree with Ava and Zachary," Alex added.

Edward sat back against the wall looking at the ground in deep thought.

"Is he okay?" Alex asked.

"Shhh, he is thinking," Zachary said.

An hour had passed, and Edward was still in the same position sitting against the wall.

Edward glanced up at his three friends. He studied them for a moment when suddenly he got an idea.

"Guy's, not sure if this plan will work but let me tell you, and then tell me what you think," Edward said.

They saw the twinkle in Edward's eyes and his confident smile.

"So what is it? Don't keep us in suspense," Zachary begged.

"Well first of all, I would like to use our individual abilities to make this escape possible. Zachary, you have an uncanny ability to get under one's skin."

Zachary nodded his head in agreement. "You got that right," Zachary said.

"Ava, you have excellent memory and can get us back towards the village."

Ava smiled at Edward's accurate assessment.

"Alex, you are tough, and we will definitely need to rely on your toughness."

Alex was also pleased with Edward's praise.

"Whatever you need to be lifted or broken. I am here for you guys," Alex said.

"So, what's the plan?" Ava asked.

Before Edward could answer, one of the guards walked over towards their prison cell. He stopped in front of their cell and laughed at them. The guard then went over to the other cells and taunted the other prisoners.

"Okay guys, where was I?" Edward asked.

"You were telling us about your plan," Ava said.

"Oh yes, Ava would you be able to get the guards to give us a bite to eat and drink?"

"Why yes, but I am not sure why," she said.

"I want you to be pleasant and polite. Be yourself."

"Okay, I can do that," she said.

"Zachary, the next part is where you come in. Once we get the food, I want you to do what you do best, and be obnoxious. I want you to pretend the food is making you sick. Once the guards come over to investigate, I want you and Ava to try to get one of the jail keys off of the guard."

Ava, Alex, and Zachary leaned in closely as they listened to Edward's plan. Their eyes lit up with anticipation to what Edward said.

Edward continued. "Now, there will be a slight problem from here. We will have one of the guards keys, but we want to make sure he is not the one trying to lock us back in for he will surely realize his keys are missing."

"That would be a problem," Alex said.

"Leave it to me," Ava said. "I will figure something out. Trust me once I have the keys they are not going to realize they were missing," Ava said confidently.

"Okay, sounds good. Once the guards are back to guarding the main door, we will need Zachary to stand on Alex's shoulders to open our cell," Edward said.

"Sounds like an excellent plan, but what do we do once the gate is open?" Ava asked Edward.

"We will use the power of Alex. Do you think you can knock over those guards or at least one of them?" Edward asked Alex.

"I sure can. I can smash the best of them," Alex said as he puffed out his chest.

"The rest of us I believe can take care of the other guard," Edward said. "Let's get ready to implement operation escape fruit," he said with a broad smile. Edward put his hand out, and others put their hands on top of Edward's. "We came here together, and we are leaving here together," Edward said.

Ava was about to get the guards attention when a voice came from an adjacent prison cell.

"What will you do when you get outside of the prison doors and have to make it out of the castle with all of King Nutty's soldiers and guards?" The mysterious voice asked.

"Where is that voice coming from?" Ava asked.

"I am in the cell next to you," the mysterious voice

rapped on the wall to indicate his location. "I can help you in this dilemma."

"How can you help us?" Zachary said, his voice filled with distrust.

"Let me introduce myself. I am Prince Chip and my father is the rightful ruler of this part of the country. My father has been imprisoned and I was caught leading a resistance against King Nutty."

"A prince, wow!" Ava said.

The prince continued.

"If you fruits succeed in getting the keys from the guards you will be able to release me and I to release some of my followers who are also imprisoned here. Once I am released, I can help you overwhelm the guards. We must make sure the guards do not alert the others of our escape. The element of surprise should be our ally. Do you fruits agree?"

The four friends nodded in agreement with what Prince Chip had said.

"Prince Chip, we agree with you, and will help you once the keys have been retrieved," Edward said.

"Very well, good luck," Prince Chip said.

"Okay, are we ready to put this plan into action?" Edward asked.

"We are," they all said as they put their hands on Edward's hand.

"Let's do this," Edward said as the four friends raised their hands in unison.

Ava was the first one up. She cleared her throat and with a quiet and sweet soft voice called for the guards.

"Excuse me; can you come down here please?" Ava said as she waved one of her arms out from the prison bars.

The guard grumbled as he walked down to their prison cell.

"Yeah, what do you want?" the guard hissed through missing teeth.

"Sir, we are super hungry. We have had nothing to eat. Would you please be able to give us some food?" Ava said in a sweet voice.

"No food for you guys," the guard snapped.

"But sir, you would not let us go without eating before our unfortunate day before King Nutty, would you?" Ava asked.

The guard studied Ava and the rest of the fruits who were lying on the ground pretending to be hungry.

The guard let out a big sigh. He saw no harm in giving them some food.

"Okay, I will see what I can get you," he said.

Ava followed the guard with her eyes. When he was out of hearing range she turned to her friends. They were all smiling at her.

Ava's friends gave her a hug.

"We are not out of the grocery isle yet. We have a ways to go before congratulations are in order," she said.

"Well said," Prince Chip said from the other side of the wall.

After several minutes had passed, the guard came back with four bowls. He opened the gate and slid four bowls on the floor.

"Enjoy," he said as he closed the prison gate.

The four of them stared at the oozing creamy colored concoction that was placed in front of them.

"I don't think I will need to fake being sick," Zachary said as he turned his nose away from the mystery bowl of food.

Alex dipped his finger in the food and tasted the creamy colored food. "Guys it's not so bad. I am not saying great but not so bad," Alex said.

Without utensils to eat, Alex picked up the bowl and tipped it towards his mouth taking a few gulps of the soupy food.

"Do you even know what it is?" Zachary said as he scrunched up his face.

Alex shook his head.

"Remember our plan," Edward interrupted.

Zachary looked at Edward and then at the bowl of food.

"I guess I will take one for the team," as he reluctantly raised the bowl to his mouth.

Zachary who was still hungry from earlier was surprised at how it tasted.

"It's pretty sweet, just how I like my food," Zachary said as he greedily devoured most of his food.

"Don't eat too fast or you might get sick," Ava warned.

"He won't get sick Ava, he has an iron stomach. He can eat almost anything," Edward said.

Zachary held up his finger to get their attention.

"Operation Zachary the awesome is about to begin," he said with a big grin.

As he grinned he let some of his food ooze from his mouth. He took the rest of the food in the bowl and flung it on the walls of the cell. Zachary laid on his side and started to groan.

"Guys it's your turn now to get some help," Zachary said.

Zachary started to groan louder as he kicked his feet about.

Ava, Edward and Alex called for the guards.

"Someone help my friend. I think he is sick!" Ava yelled.

"Help! Help!" Edward and Alex yelled.

They could hear the guards running down to their cell.

"What's going on?" they demanded.

"Our friend, I think what he ate did not agree with him," Ava said pointing to Zachary.

The guards looked at each other dumbfounded.

"What do we do?" one of the guards asked the other.

The guards opened up the gate and bent down to help Zachary up. As they reached over to help Zachary, Ava grabbed the keys off of the toothless guard. Zachary, seeing that Ava had the key pretended he needed a beverage desperately.

"Thanks for helping me but I need something to drink fast," he said pretending to cough.

"Get him some milk fast," the one guard said to the other guard.

The toothless and slow guard moved as fast as he could which was not fast at all. He returned with a cup of milk for Zachary. Zachary drank the milk in one big swig. He cleared his throat and began to feel better.

"Thanks, you guys are a life saver. Milk hit the spot," Zachary said.

"You must be careful and slow down when you eat," the one guard lectured.

"Yes, yes," Zachary answered.

Ava talked with the toothless guard as he and the other guard closed the gate. Ava wanted to make sure the toothless guard did not know his keys were missing. As she continued to talk with her soft voice and big smile, the other guard locked up their gate. The guards walked back to their post not realizing they had been played.

Ava, with a big smile on her face held the keys triumphantly up in her hands.

"Fruit's that was awesome!" Alex said proudly.

"You must hurry, quickly. No time to rest on your laurels, you can celebrate after we escape," Prince Chip said.

Agreeing with the prince's advice, Ava handed the keys to Zachary.

"Remember, be quiet," Ava said.

"Ava and Edward, you guys be on the lookout for us as me and Alex try to get this gate opened," Zachary said.

Alex and Zachary walked over to the prison gate while Edward and Ava watched the guards.

"Here hold the keys while I climb on you," Zachary said as he handed Alex the cell keys.

Zachary proceeded to climb on top of Alex's shoulders. He held one hand on the prison bars to get his balance and with his other hand reached for the keys from Alex.

"Okay Alex, hand me the keys," he said.

Alex handed Zachary the keys with one hand while he held onto the back of one of Zachary's legs. After retrieving the keys from Alex, Zachary wanted to make sure that the coast was clear.

"Hey guys, is the coast is clear?" he asked in a low voice.

Edward and Ava who were already on the lookout raised their hands up signaling the coast was indeed clear.

"It's a go. Edward and Ava have given the go sign," Alex said to Zachary.

Zachary while trying to hold his balance carefully maneuvered the keys through the bars. His hands steady as he put the key in the hole.

"How's it going up there?" Alex asked.

Zachary kicked Alex's head to be quiet. Zachary with his long arms turned the key and with a slight pop sound opened the gate. Zachary quickly jumped down from Alex.

"Okay guys, let's get out of here," Zachary said, his voice filled with excitement.

They were all excited and scared. This was their chance to get out of the prison.

"Fruits I love you," Edward said as they all embraced.

"Okay, let's free Prince Chip," Ava said.

"Prince Chip we are coming to get you," Edward said to the prince.

"Excellent, now hurry before they realize what has happened," the prince said.

The four friends quietly exited their cell while they watched the guards whose backs were turned to them. They reached Prince Chip's cell. He was standing at the front of the prison bars. Prince Chip held his finger to his mouth indicating for them to be quiet. To their surprise Prince Chip was extremely tall. He was taller than most of the cookies the fruits had encountered.

Zachary handed Prince Chip the keys, who quickly unlocked the gate, but before letting himself out he asked the four friends to come in.

"You cannot stand out in the open. Let's finish our

planning in here where they can't spot you," Prince Chip instructed.

The four friends stared blankly at Prince Chip.

"Trust me. You can't stand out in the open too long," Prince Chip said.

One of the guards began to fidget and started looking around. The four friends quickly ran into the prison cell with Prince Chip. The guard resumed talking to his partner.

"That was close," Ava said.

They all nodded their heads in agreement.

"Thanks guys," Prince Chip said as he extended out his hand. "Please quickly introduce yourselves."

The four friends quickly introduced themselves to Prince Chip.

"Please to meet you four heroes, now let's finish your plan," he said to Edward.

Prince Chip turned his attention to Alex.

"I believe you and I can take care of the guards. Don't you think?"

Alex looked over at the guards who were laughing at each other's farts.

"I can take one of the guards, the one with the missing teeth," Alex said confidently.

Prince Chip smiled at Alex's toughness.

"Alex we do not have much time once we leave this prison cell. We need to make sure those guards do not set the alarm. Take a look at the red button on the wall to the right of the second guard. We must not let them hit the red button. Do you understand?"

Alex's face was serious.

"I do," Alex said.

"Excellent, now Edward, Ava and Zachary once Alex and I are subduing the guards please start unlocking the other prison cells. My fellow chips who are imprisoned with me will be released and will help me rescue my father and we will have enough power to get you out of the castle. Once you're out of the castle you will be on your own; for I and my fellow chips will fight to get back the castle that belongs to my family. Are you ready my friends?"

"Yes," they said in unison.

"Now, let's go subdue the guards and release the rest of the prisoners."

Chapter 12

The five of them left Prince Chip's cell. As Alex and Prince Chip headed towards the guards Edward, Zachary and Ava waited. Prince Chip gave Alex the go sign.

Alex and Prince Chip raced towards the unsuspecting guards. Prince Chip jumped on one of the guards knocking him out but the toothless guard seeing his partner knocked over raced towards the red alarm button.

"Alex get him!" Prince Chip yelled.

Alex ran as fast as his little legs could go. The toothless guard was about to reach for the button when Alex leapt into the air and tackled him.

"Guys, start unlocking the prisoners," Prince Chip said to Edward, Zachary and Ava.

Zachary who was handling the keys moved quickly towards the other prison cells, with Edward and Ava following closely behind. Zachary tossed the keys into one of the prison cells. One of the cookies grabbed the keys and unlocked the gate. The two cookies rushed out of the cell and began unlocking three other gates. A total of eight cookies had been released and they were standing near Prince Chip, smiling and shaking his hand.

"The thanks my friends are not for me but for our four fruit friends. Their bravery I will always remember," Prince Chip said to his comrades.

The eight escaped cookies thanked the four friends whole heartedly. Prince Chip instructed two of his cookies to lock up the guards. As the cookies locked up the guards Prince Chip turned to his four new friends.

"You have held up your end of the bargain, now I will do the same. I will get you out of the castle, but like I said, once you leave you are on your own."

"So what's the next step?" Edward asked Prince Chip.

"I believe a diversion is in order."

"A what?" Zachary asked.

"A diversion dummy," Edward said.

"Boys let's be nice," Ava said.

"I will lead you out of the castle. I know all the secret passage ways in my father's castle," Prince Chip said.

"Now soldiers, I want you to round up as much

resistance as you can. You are some of my best fighters and I need you to get more of the prisoners freed. You guys will need to create as much havoc as you can so King Nutty and his cookies do not know what hit them. Make sure you lock up as many of King Nutty's guards, soldiers and friends as possible. Once I return from getting our friends out of here we will set our sights on freeing my father, the real king and taking the castle back completely."

The soldiers saluted Prince Chip.

"Okay, now go," Prince Chip ordered his eight covert cookies.

The eight cookies quickly and quietly opened the door and left.

"My fruit friends, let's go. A secret passageway leads out of the castle," Prince Chip said as he waved the four friends to follow him.

Prince Chip and the four friends silently maneuvered around large pillars making sure they were not spotted. They came to a large open area and hid behind one of the large pillars. In the open area were several of King Nutty's soldiers standing guard.

Prince Chip leaned down to the four friends.

"On the other side that there is a long corridor?" he said pointing in from of them.

They nodded their heads in agreement.

"There is a fountain of milk at the end of the corridor. I need you guys to get to the fountain, once at the fountain I need you to turn the golden statue next to the fountain. Once you turn the statue, a wall behind the fountain will open up leading to a secret passageway out of here."

Prince Chip was about to continue when Edward interrupted him.

"You're not coming with us to make sure we make it out of the castle," Edward said.

Ava, Alex and Zachary looked at Prince Chip for his response.

"You are correct Edward. I can't make it out with you."

"You gave your word," Zachary replied.

Prince Chip nodded his head.

Prince pointed in the direction of King Nutty's guards. "You cannot escape from the guards unless I stay behind and distract them. Once they come after me you guys will be able to make it to the fountain and to your freedom."

"But won't you get caught?" Ava insisted.

"I will not. I know this castle like the back of my hand and I can take care of myself," Prince Chip paused for a moment, and gave a big sigh. "Friends, you will always be remembered in my father's kingdom as heroes. You will be legends in the Aisle of Cookies. The healthy ones that helped defeat the tyranny of King Nutty, and I can't thank you enough but I can give you something to take to an old friend of my fathers. A grapefruit named Ebenezer."

The four friends stood in shock at the name of Ebenezer.

Edward was the first to speak up. "You know Ebenezer?"

"Not as well as my father. All I am sure off is my father said he was very important to the cause."

"What cause Ava asked?"

"Not sure my father did not tell me. Once you go through the secret passageway you will find a hidden panel on the left side of the wall. You need one person to step on the seventh brick on the left side of the secret passage and another person stepping on the seventh brick on the right side of the secret passage at the same time. A panel will open up. Take the bag to Ebenezer. He will understand what the content in the bag means. No time to discuss. Get moving."

Alex came up to Prince Chip without saying a word and gave him a big hug. Edward, Ava and Zachary also gave the prince a hug.

"Wait until the guards chase after me. Once they start chasing me make a run for the fountain of milk."

"King Nutty's soldiers smell like dirty underwear!" he yelled.

Prince Chip started running.

"Get him!" the guards yelled as they chased after Prince Chip.

Seeing the guards chase after Prince Chip the four of them ran across the open area into the corridor. As they made their way down the long corridor they spotted the fountain of milk.

"There's the fountain of milk," Zachary shouted.

"Okay, let's hurry up," Edward said as he glanced over his shoulder.

"Relax chief. No one is coming," Zachary said.

"Alex, you're the strongest. Can you turn the golden statue?" Edward asked.

"I can sure try," Alex said as he grabbed onto the statue.

Alex turned the statue with ease and the wall behind the fountain slowly opened. As the wall opened up, one of King Nutty's soldiers jumped out.

"Got you!" the soldier said to the shocked fruits.

The soldier reached for Ava. As he grabbed Ava's arm

she grabbed the soldier's other arm and flipped him on his back. The soldier hit the floor hard, knocking him unconscious.

"Never put your hands on a lady," Ava said triumphantly.

Edward, Zachary and Alex stood in disbelief.

"Close your mouth boys, we need to get out of here," she said.

"You know karate?" Edward said to Ava.

"Aikido, and a lady does not reveal everything," she said with a slight smile.

Zachary looked down at the unconscious soldier.

"Darn she might be able to beat you up Alex."

"I am glad Ava and I are friends," Alex said.

"Come on guys, we need to find the secret panel," Ava said as she counted seven steps. "Remember we need to step on the right bricks at the same time."

Edward counted out to the seventh brick across from Ava.

"Ready?" Edward asked Ava.

"Ready," Ava replied.

"On the count of three we step on the bricks," Edward instructed.

Edward and Ava counted to three and stepped on their

bricks at the same time. The secret passageway shook, and on a wall next to were Edward was standing, a hidden panel opened up revealing a red velvet bag.

"Edward grab the bag and let's get out of here," Ava said.

Ava raced down the corridor followed by Alex and Zachary. Edward grabbed the bag. He felt an odd shape object inside. Edward ran after his friend's carefully holding the velvet bag.

The four of them raced down the long corridor.

"How long is this tunnel? I have been running forever," Alex huffed.

"I think just a little bit further," Ava said.

Ava slowed down and waited for her friends. She pointed to an opening in the tunnel.

The four friends walked thru the opening, they were excited and nervous at the same time. They walked along a large green pasture. The sky with its marshmallow clouds and a Sunkist sun beamed down on them.

"We made it!" exclaimed Zachary.

"We sure did!" Edward said as they high fived each other.

"Fruits, hey fruits," Alex said trying to get the attention of his friends.

Before Alex had a chance to explain what he was see-ing, a large explosion sounded.

Edward, Zachary and Ava turned around.

"King Nutty's castle!" Edward exclaimed.

"You mean King Chip's castle," Ava reminded them.

They saw smoke coming from the castle.

"I hope Prince Chip succeeds. That King Nutty is a horrible cookie," Ava said.

"Prince Chip will win," Edward said confidently.

"How can you be so sure?" Alex asked.

"Something is different about the castle from when we first arrived," Edward said smiling.

Zachary, Ava and Alex studied the castle.

"Not sure what you are seeing bro, same dirty castle to me," Zachary said.

Alex also did not see a difference, but Ava did.

"Edward you have good eyes," she said.

"What are you guys talking about? Did you drink some special juice or something?" Zachary said annoyed.

Ava pointed to the large flag that was waving at the top of the castle.

"When we first approached that flag had a pretty ugly picture of King Nutty. Now the flag is replaced with a flag of a golden dragon," she said.

"So, what's your point?" Zachary asked.

"Her point is if King Nutty's flag is down and replaced with a different flag, which means Prince Chip has won the battle, and has restored his father to the throne," Alex said triumphantly.

"He is one tough cookie," Zachary said.

"I guess this is the end of our trip to the Aisle of Cookies, time to head back home," Edward said.

"How do we get back?" Alex asked.

"Hey Ava, you said you remembered the way back home right?" Edward asked.

Ava tried to figure out the right direction.

"No, I said I knew how to get back to the village of the healthy cookies but we got all turned around. Not sure how to get back from here. The only thing familiar thing is the large mountain over there," she said pointing to the east.

The other three fruits looked over at the mountain.

"That's it!" exclaimed Edward. "The mountain is near the marsh when we first came out of the cavern.

"You're right! We head towards the mountain and we should be back home," Ava said.

Chapter 13

The four friends headed in the direction towards the marsh. They talked about their adventure and their escape from King Nutty. They were excited to come home and tell everybody their wild and crazy adventure.

"What do you think is in the bag?" Zachary asked Edward.

Edward stopped. He held up the bag unsure on what to do. "Should we be looking in the bag? Whatever is inside is for Ebenezer," Edward said.

"What's with the mysterious grapefruit anyway," Alex added.

"I don't see the harm Edward of at least peeking in the bag," Ava said.

Alex and Zachary agreed with Ava. Edward with his scientific mind was also interested. Edward nodded in agreement with his friends. He slowly opened the bag and peeked in.

Zachary, Alex, and Ava leaned toward Edward in anticipation. Edward's eyes bulged at what was inside the bag.

"Come on Edward tell us what's in the bag," Zachary begged.

Without saying a word, Edward reached into the bag and pulled out a wooden statue of a peach girl painted vibrant pink with green colors.

"Ava is that you?" Alex asked.

Edward, Zachary and Alex looked at the statue and then back at Ava.

Ava stared at the statue. She turned towards Edward. "This is like the plum statue."

"Yes this statue is similar to the plum statue but why is there one of you?" Edward asked.

"That's the million dollar question," Zachary added. "This place is beginning to freak me out. "Let's get out of this weird world and back home," Zachary suggested.

Edward, Alex, and Ava agreed with Zachary. They needed to get home.

Edward put the statue of the peach girl back in the bag. The four friends entered the woods near the mountain where they first entered the Aisle of Cookies.

"The marsh is close," Ava said.

The excitement of them being one step closer to home continued to build, except Edward who remained curiously quiet.

"Edward, you have not said much lately. What's up?" Ava said intuitively.

"Something the elder said in the village right before we got caught by King Nutty."

"What did the Elder say," Ava asked.

"I don't know. I can't remember what he said. Do any of you remember?" Edward asked.

Zachary and Alex could not remember what the elder said.

"Do you think it is important?" Alex asked.

"I hope not," Edward responded.

"Come on guys we are almost home. Edward, stop worrying about nothing," Zachary said as he playfully punched Edward in the arm.

Edward agreed with his yellow friend.

"Okay, we are almost home," Edward said excitedly.

They came across the opening in the woods, the mountain jutted out of the marsh stood majestically in front of them.

They hugged each other, giddy with delight.

"Once we get to the mountain we are home free!" Edward shouted.

The four of them went into the marsh. As they inched closer to the mountain, a dark swarm approached.

"Oh fruit! Not again!" Zachary shouted.

They raced away from the dark swarming mass towards the mountain.

"The swarm is gaining on us!" Ava shouted.

"We're almost......" Edward stomped in mid-sentence as he saw in from of them a large whirlpool.

The water became rougher as Edward started to feel himself get dragged towards the swirling water.

"What's going on Edward?" Zachary asked.

"I think we are in real trouble here," Edward said.

The three other friends saw the whirlpool.

"So what Edward, just move through, we need to get past those fruit flies," Zachary responded.

"Not a smart idea. I think this might be what the elder was talking about," Edward said.

The whirlpool grew in intensity; a blue glow at the center of the swirling water. The whirlpool began to suck them in. They tried to escape the whirlpool when all of a sudden a bright flash of light hit the whirlpool. The whirlpool vanished.

The four friends stood at the base of the mountain.

"That was close," Edward said.

"You ain't kidding," Zachary said.

"Guys that swarm of fruit flies are still coming for us," Alex said as he pointed to the dark buzzing swarm.

"That's not our only problem. The mountain is fading," Ava said.

The four friends looked at the mountain. The mountain was losing its solidity.

"Guys we need to get to the opening at the base of the mountain before the mountain vanishes," Edward said.

Zachary, Alex, and Ava did not argue. The four friends raced towards the mountain as the swarm of fruit flies gave chase.

"The mountain is getting even lighter. Are we going to make it Edward?" Ava asked.

"I hope so," Edward said.

"What happens if we don't make it?" Alex asked.

"You don't want to know," Edward said.

"Enough with the questions," Zachary said.

As the mountain began to vanish, and the swarm of fruit flies about to descend, the four friends they jumped into the mountain opening. In another flash of bright light, the mountain disappeared, and the four became unconscious.

Chapter 14

Edward, Zachary, Ava and Alex woke up in the woods. A car honked in the distance.

Zachary the first to stand up leaned over his friends. "Guys get up," he said.

Edward, Ava and Alex slowly got up.

"I guess we are not bread," Zachary said.

They all nodded their heads in agreement.

"Where are we?" Alex asked.

The car again gave another honk.

"Not sure. Let's go find out where the honking is coming from," Edward said.

The four of them walked through the woods.

"This sure is not Aisle of the Cookies," Zachary said looking at a rock he picked up.

The honking of the horn could be heard again.

"The sound is coming from over there," Edward said as he walked faster.

The four of them reached an open field.

The sound of the honking horn grew louder.

"I can't believe my eyes!" Edward exclaimed.

Ava, Alex, and Zachary stood beside Edward.

"We are home!" Zachary shouted.

Zachary raced towards the bus.

Edward, Ava and Alex chased after Zachary. The four friends screamed with delight as they raced towards the bus. The bus door opened and instead of the avocado bus driver greeting them it was Ebenezer Grapefruit.

"Welcome home! Hope your adventure was fun and exciting," Ebenezer said.

Ebenezer glanced at the bag Edward was holding.

"So young man, a souvenir from the Aisle of Cookies?" Ebenezer asked Edward.

Edward not sure how to interpret the events to Ebenezer, decided to pull out the statue and hand it to him.

Ebenezer's eyes widened at the sight of the statue.

Zachary spoke up. "We are supposed to give you this statue from Prince Chip and his dad the king. Where else have you been?" Zachary asked.

Ebenezer gave a hearty laugh.

"Once you four are rested I have an adventure you

might be interested in," Ebenezer said with a twinkle in his eyes.

Edward, Ava, Zachary and Alex smiled at each other as the boarded the city bus for home.

About Author

D. J. Mincy has been writing for over fifteen years. Adventures of Apple & Banana is his first published children's book. He lives with his daughter Ava.

CPSIA information can be obtained at www.ICGtesting.com
Printed in the USA
BVOW07s0233241013

334502BV00001B/89/P